NIGHT DANCER

Mythical Piper of the

Native American Southwest

By **MARCIA VAUGHAN**

Illustrated by **LISA DESIMINI**

Orchard Books · New York
An Imprint of Scholastic Inc.

Text copyright © 2002 Marcia Vaughan
Illustrations copyright © 2002 Lisa Desimini

All rights reserved. Published by Orchard Books, an imprint of Scholastic Inc. ORCHARD BOOKS and
design are registered trademarks of Orchard Books, Inc., a subsidiary of Scholastic Inc. SCHOLASTIC
and associated logos are trademarks and/or registered trademarks of Scholastic Inc.

Library of Congress Cataloging-in-Publication Data available.
ISBN 0-439-35248-7

10 9 8 7 6 5 4 3 2 1   02 03 04 05 06

Printed in Singapore 46
First edition, October 2002
The text type is set in Gilgamesh Book.
Book design by David Caplan

For my Mom and Dad
—L. D.

For my favorite desert-dwellers,
Susan Pearson-Davis and Daniel Davis,
who introduced me to Kokopelli
—M. V.

As moonlight washes across the canyon, a figure as old as time steps from the rocks and raises his flute. Kokopelli, the mystical musician of the Rio Grande, plays an ancient melody, inviting all desert-dwellers to join his jubilant dance.

Luminous moon, bursting with light, sweeps the darkness from the desert night.

Shadows grow. Shadows stretch.

One shadow leaps in sprightly steps.

Kokopelli!

Merry minstrel of the night. He lifts his flute and pipes a tune.

Come dance, come dance, come dance with me
Stepping and stamping joyously.
Like the stars and the wind, happy and free,
Who'll dance away the night with me?

Sweet song. Secret song. Echoes off canyon walls,
rushes through arroyos, whispers past the pueblo.

Atop the cliff, Coyote listens. She tosses back her head and howls, "I will dance with you on this desert night, stepping and stamping in the moon-bright light."

Sweeping her tail from side to side, Coyote climbs nimbly down the cliff to join the night dancer.

And Kokopelli dances along, leaping and laughing and playing his song.

Come dance, come dance, come dance with me
Sliding and gliding gleefully.
Like the stars and the wind, happy and free,
Who'll dance away the night with me?

Curled beneath a rock, Snake awakes and shakes his rattles. "I will dance with you on this desert night, sliding and gliding in the moon-bright light."

Rattling his scaly tail, Snake follows Moon's silver trail and joins the night dancers. Kokopelli dances along, leaping and laughing and playing his song.

Come dance, come dance, come dance with me
Snapping and clapping playfully.
Like the stars and the wind, happy and free,
Who'll dance away the night with me?

In the moonlight, Tortoise's shell glistens as she listens to the music floating on the still night air. "I will dance with you on this desert night, snapping and clapping in the moon-bright light."

Tortoise brushes past the prickly pears as she shuffles over to join the night dancers.

Kokopelli dances along, leaping and laughing and playing his song.

Come dance, come dance, come dance with me
Romping and stomping merrily.
Like the stars and the wind, happy and free,
Who'll dance away the night with me?

In the arroyo, Javelina, timid and shy, lifts her ears toward the starry sky. "I will dance with you on this desert night, romping and stomping in the moon-bright light." Shaking her bristly coat, Javelina trots down the trail to join the night dancers. Kokopelli dances along, leaping and laughing and playing his song.

Come dance, come dance, come dance with me
Whirling and twirling jubilantly.
Like the stars and the wind, happy and free,
Who'll dance away the night with me?

Deep in the canyon, Jackrabbit, tail a-quiver, jumps up and answers the piper's song. "I will dance with you on this desert night, whirling and twirling in the moon-bright light." He zigs and zags around the red-baked rocks, rushing to join the night dancers. And Kokopelli dances along, leaping and laughing and playing his song.

Come dance, come dance, come dance with me
Spinning and grinning cheerfully.
Like the stars and the wind, happy and free,
Who'll dance away the night with me?

Beyond the tumbleweeds, Tarantula creeps on many legs. She pauses as a thread of music wraps itself around her. "I will dance with you on this desert night, spinning and grinning in the moon-bright light."

Tarantula tiptoes through the tumbleweeds and joins Kokopelli, Coyote, Snake, Tortoise, Javelina, and Jackrabbit in their night dance.

Past the slumbering pueblo, Kokopelli dances along,
leaping and laughing and playing his song.

In their beds, the children dream of a magic man.
Who can it be?
They wake and see
Kokopelli!

Stepping and stamping. Sliding and gliding. They follow the piper into the night.

Snapping and clapping. Romping and stomping. They dance through the desert in the moon-bright light.

Kokopelli spins with a step and a hop.

Whirling and twirling to the mesa top.

Cacti sway. Shadows play.

Dancers dance the night away.

Then all at once the music stops.
Silence echoes off canyon walls, hushes through arroyos,
whispers past the pueblo.

Rising Sun, bursting with light, sweeps away the desert night.
Dancers yawn, dancers stretch. They turn for home with tired steps.
Sleepy Moon rolls from sight, as Kokopelli, merry minstrel of the
night, lifts his flute for one last song.

Let morning awake and the new day begin
For when the Moon shines bright, I'll dance again.

And Kokopelli's song drifts away on the wind.

Meet Kokopelli

Kokopelli is found in the mythology of the Hopi, Zuni, and Pueblo peoples of the desert regions of the American Southwest. He is a humpbacked being with supernatural abilities who plays many roles.

In legends of the Pueblo people, Kokopelli is a minstrel who brings music and dance. He wanders the desert playing his flute. On his back he carries a sack of songs, and trades new ones for old as he travels. In Navajo mythology, Kokopelli is a hunter who plays his flute to lure mountain sheep close to the human hunters. The Zuni depict Kokopelli as a priest who brings clouds and rain to ensure good crops.

Ancient images of Kokopelli are found on canyon walls, pottery, and baskets, and in ceremonial chambers. He appears performing activities that are essential to human life: dancing; hunting; trading; and bringing music, gifts, rain, and fertility to the people and their crops.

Although Kokopelli's role and appearance vary from area to area, he is usually shown as a dancing humpbacked figure playing a flute. Atop his head is a headdress of feathers. He often carries a pack filled with gifts for the people.

Most people believe that the name "Kokopelli" is a combination of "koko," the Zuni word for "rain people," and "pelli," which in Hopi means "hump" or "hemisphere."

Kokopelli's role as a spiritual being is dramatized through myths, legends, rituals, ceremonies, and dances. He serves as a mediator between people and nature. His activities help ensure a plentiful life as they foster a bountiful relationship between humans and their world.

From ancient times to the present, native peoples consider Kokopelli to be a celebrant of life . . . the pied piper of the Rio Grande.